SESAME STREET
123

BUSY MONSTERS

we make books come alive®

pi kids **Phoenix International Publications, Inc.**
Chicago • London • New York • Hamburg • Mexico City • Sydney

Illustrated by Bob Berry, Tom Brannon, Warner McGee, and Sesame Workshop

Customer Service: 1-877-277-9441 or customerservice@pikidsmedia.com

Published by Phoenix International Publications, Inc.
8501 West Higgins Road   59 Gloucester Place
Chicago, Illinois 60631   London W1U 8JJ

PI Kids and *we make books come alive* are trademarks of Phoenix International Publications, Inc., and are registered in the United States.

Look and Find is a trademark of Phoenix International Publications, Inc., and is registered in the United States and Canada.

www.pikidsmedia.com

ISBN: 978-1-5037-5454-6

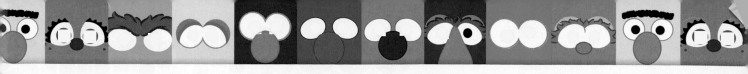

Table of Contents

Good Morning

Wake Up, !

The is up, but isn't, until...**STRUMMM! COOOO!**

"What's making all that noise?" wonders. He hops out of

bed to find out.

Outside, a cheery is shining down on and .

"It's a great day," says . "I just had to play a song to let

everybody know!"

While  **STRUMS** his , a  starts to **COO**.

"Wow!" says . "The  is singing along."

---

picture key

Elmo	sun	Ernie	Bert	guitar	pigeon

 sings along too, until...**BOINGGG!**

 hears a kid on a . **BOING!** He hears the .

STRUM! He hears the . **COO!** And he hears his friend

, sounding sad.

"Oh dear," says . "I, , would like to make a noise

too. But sadly, my will not hoot anymore."

 hears another noise. **HONKKK!** That gives him an idea!

picture key

				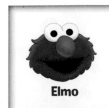	
Elmo	pogo stick	guitar	pigeon	Grover	horn

follows the noise down the street, until...**CLANGGG!**

 **CLANGS** the of his trash can. And he **HONKS**

a different kind of .

", would you share your with so he can

make some noise too?" asks.

"Well, all right," says , handing the  to .

"The more noise the better!"

 HONKS his . **CLANKS** his .

 CLAPS his to join in!

" is glad he lives on such a noisy

street,"  says. "Otherwise  might

have stayed asleep and missed

a great morning!"

picture key

Elmo	**Oscar**	**lid**	**horn**	**Grover**	**hands**

Look and Find

Goodbye, Mommy! Goodbye, Daddy! Now it's time to go to school. Find these things Elmo will see in and around his classroom:

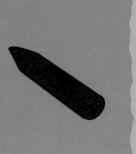

Let's Pretend!

Hooray! It's story time at school! Miss Bridget reads a funny

to  and his friends.

"Once upon a time, a little monster found a special pair of .

She put them on and could not stop dancing! But she had chores to

do. She danced over to the farmer to buy some . Then she

danced over to the baker to sell the .

"But wait! One of the 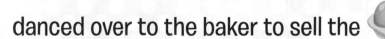 was a golden ! The baker said

the golden belonged to the giant, who had a golden ."

picture key

book	Elmo	shoes	eggs	egg	duck

"Then what happens?" asks . So Miss Bridget turns

the page of the  and reads some more.

"The dancing monster danced up, up,

up a beanstalk to give the golden

to the giant. The giant was fast asleep, so

the dancing monster asked a musician to

play the  and wake him up.

"The giant was so happy, he threw a party. The baker brought

lots of . After the party, the little monster was too tired

to dance home. So the giant called

a , and the monster got

home safe and sound! Everybody

lived happily ever after."

picture key

| Elmo | book | egg | violin | pizza | taxi |

As the story ends, the rings for recess!

At recess, pretends to be a dancer with special .

 pretends to be a farmer gathering .

 pretends to be a baker who bakes .

 pretends to be a musician who plays .

 pretends to drive a .

"What are you pretending to be, ?" asks .

 climbs up, up, up to the top of the slide and calls down,

"Fee-fi-fo-fum, 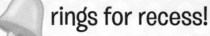 is a GIANT. Here he comes!"

picture key

bell	Zoe	shoes	Grover	eggs	Cookie Monster
pizza	Big Bird	violin	Abby	taxi	Elmo

Look and Find®

"Ah, yes, greetings! It is I, the Count, in the Wild Wild West with Elmo and Grover. I can't stop counting, even when I'm pretending to be a cowboy! Can you count in the scene along with me?"

1 cowboy hat

2 sheriff's stars

3 cactus plants

4 cowboy boots

5 lovely lizards

Fun with Friends

I'm so glad we're friends, Elmo.

Elmo is glad too. It's fun to do things with a friend.

Friends have fun swimming at the beach together.

Friends have fun searching for treasure together.

Friends have fun playing in the sand together.

Uh, Ernie? Can I take a turn now?

My Pal

Someone on Sesame Street is having a surprise birthday party!

Usually hates surprises, and birthdays, and parties. But

this surprise birthday party is different. It's for his friend !

 lifts the of his and looks around. He

wants to find the perfect to bring to the party.

"What's in this pile of ?" says . "Maybe there's

something grimy for . Hey, and grimy rhyme. I'll

write a birthday poem for my pal!"

picture key

Slimey	Oscar	lid	trash can	present	trash

 searches Sesame Street for more rhymes. At the pool,

he sees a kid with a toy , and sitting in a .

 says, " and  are rhymes."

At the park, sees a big , and he sees his

reflection in a puddle. "  rhymes with ME," says .

Then  looks at his . It is time for the party!

picture key

Oscar	boat	Bert	float	tree	watch

"Surprise!" yells everyone.  smiles. He is really surprised!

After blows out the candles on his ,  reads:

"I don't want a or a .

A pretty isn't for me.

Those things aren't gross or grimy.

But one thing I love...is my pal !"

picture key

Slimey	cake	Oscar	boat	float	tree

WHAT'S DIFFERENT?

When her friends score a point, Zoe cheers!
Spot 10 things that are different in the playground pictures.

What Is a Friend?

A friend will push your swing for you,
or push a wheelchair along.
A friend will climb to reach your kite.
A friend is someone who is **STRONG**.

A friend will teach you how to dance,
or how to make a paper heart.
A friend will read some books with you.
A friend is someone who is **SMART**.

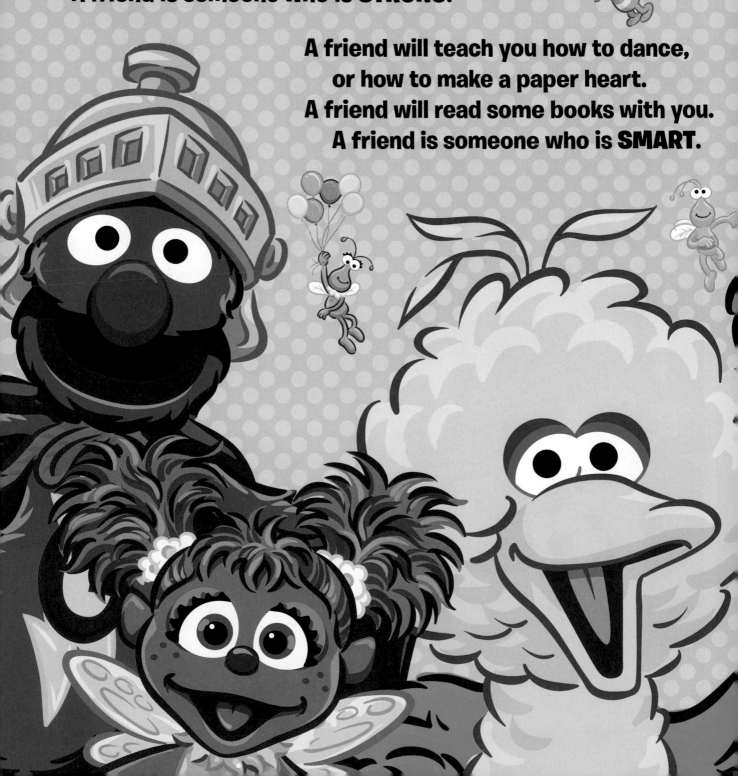

A friend will save a seat for you,
and make sure you're not left behind.
A friend will bring you picnic treats.
A friend is someone who is **KIND**.

A friend is nice to all new kids,
and has fun trying something new.
A friend is **STRONG** and **SMART** and **KIND**.
A friend is someone just like **YOU!**

A New

 is going to the park with her . "When will I

be big enough to ride a 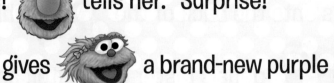?" asks.

"Today!"  tells her. "Surprise!"

 gives a brand-new purple  with a

big pink and pink , and a pink .

 is so excited! But she is also a little bit scared.

"I'll be right beside you until you are ready to ride on your

own," says.

At the park, puts on her  nice and snug.

She climbs onto her . Then she says, "Ready, set, go!"

picture key

tricycle	Zoe	Daddy	wheel	handlebars	helmet

At first, holds onto the back of the  while

pedals slowly. Then  pedals faster and faster, and before long

she tells that he can let go.

"Wheee!" shouts . "I'm flying like a !"

As  zooms along the path, she sees a friend. It's .

She is riding a , all by herself!

", when will I be big enough to ride a ?" asks.

"Soon enough," says. "And when you are, I'll be right beside

you until you are ready to ride on your own."

picture key

Daddy	**tricycle**	**Zoe**	**bird**	**Prairie Dawn**	**bicycle**

 rides her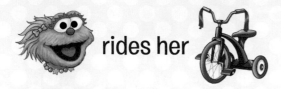

around the park for a long time.

Then 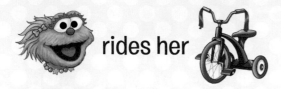 says, "It's time to

go home."

They stop at the crosswalk and wait for the walk signal as a

speedy green  zooms past.

"When will I be big enough to drive a ?"  asks.

"Soon enough," says. "Now let's cross the street. Walk

right beside me." He pushes the  with one  and holds

little  safely with the other.

"I'm big enough to ride a , and I'll be big enough to ride a

 and drive a  someday,"  tells .

"But I will never be too big to hold your ."

---

picture key

Zoe	tricycle	Daddy	car	hand	bicycle

WHAT'S DIFFERENT?

Families care, families share, and families have fun together! The Twiddlebug family is right at home in Ernie's window box. Can you find 10 differences between the pictures?

Answer key: blue flowers, Ernie's cap, Twiddlebug's flower color, blue flying Twiddlebug, yellow playhouse, yo-yo color, Twiddlebug in blue playhouse, pink balloon, green leaf, Twiddlebug in green playhouse

Let's Move

Go Away, !

 lies in , but it's hard to sleep. He is too excited

for tomorrow's trip to the water park. can't wait to ride

down the giant water and splash in the pool.

"Tomorrow is going to be the best day ever!" says as he

finally closes his .

picture key

rain	Elmo	bed	slide	wave	eyes

Morning is here! grabs his and 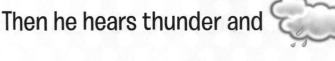.

Then he hears thunder and .

"The water park is closed today," says .

"But really wants to go to the water park and

splash in the  pool," says sadly. "

doesn't want to stay inside and do nothing."

picture key

Elmo	swimsuit	snorkel	rain	Mommy	wave

"Who says you have to stay inside?" says , handing a

 and a pair of to .

Outside, giggles as it drizzles. He splashes in a .

Then he sees something wonderful in the sky!

 chases the and says,

"Today is the best day ever!"

picture key

Mommy	coat	boots	Elmo	puddle	rainbow

Look and Find®

Let's get up and go!
It's sunny outside.
Get your wheels rolling
and go for a ride!

Count along with the Count
to find these moving things:

1 Super Grover

2 spiders

3 pigeons

4 butterflies

5 sports helmets

Sharing and Caring

Too Many !

One morning, places his trusty chef's on his head

and makes his way to the kitchen. He grabs a big , his lucky

, some flour, and some .

"Me bake !" says .

But when it comes to 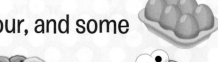, sometimes gets too

excited. "Maybe me make too many ," says . "Way,

way too many. Even for hungry monster!"

picture key

cookies	Cookie Monster	hat	bowl	spoon	eggs

 wonders what he can do with his extra .

Maybe they could be the tires on a , or the body of a

. Maybe one could be a . Maybe  could grow

on a . The whole world could be made out of !

"Mmmm," says . "Hmmm. That delicious...but not

very realistic."

 has another idea. Instead of eating all the ,

or building a whole out of , maybe he can *share*

his yummy with his friends. , , and

 think that is a great idea.

"The only thing me love more than ," says ,

"is sharing ! Om nom nom."

picture key

Cookie Monster	**cookies**	**world**	**Elmo**	**Grover**	**Zoe**

Playground games are a great time to share! Take a look at the photos and see if you can spot these things that monsters are sharing:

All About Opposites

 opens up his and starts to read. He laughs right out **LOUD**. The is really funny.

"Shhh," whispers, pointing to a . "The says '**QUIET** Please.' Other in the library are trying to read."

"Sorry," says. "I promise not to laugh anymore." picks up another . He makes a **LOUD** yelp, and jumps up in his with a **LOUD** thump. This is a little bit scary.

"Shhh," says , pointing to the again.

picture key

Ernie	Bert	book	sign	monsters	chair

At home, and  make dinner. slices

a , a , and some . Then he tosses the

veggies into a big, shiny bowl.

"Oops," says , as the , , and

tumble to the floor.

"Now the kitchen is too **MESSY**," says . He grabs a

to wash the floor and make the kitchen nice and **NEAT**.

picture key

Bert	Ernie	cucumber	pepper	carrots	mop

After dinner,  organizes his and caps.

 plays a jazzy tune on his with .

 is **LOUD** and **MESSY**. is **QUIET** and **NEAT**.

The thing likes best is to sit and sort .

likes to dance around with .

 and are very different, but there is one thing

they always agree on: they are best friends!

picture key

Bert	paper clips	bottle	Ernie	saxophone	Rubber Duckie

Look and Find®

Elmo wants to take pictures of opposites! He looks **UP** and **DOWN** and all around. Can you help Elmo find things that are:

INSIDE Elmo's room

OUTSIDE Elmo's room

ABOVE the window

BELOW the window

in **FRONT** of Elmo

BEHIND Elmo

IN the bookcase

OUT of the bookcase

Om Nom Nom

for Everyone

"**M**e love !" says . "Good thing me chef." He

puts on his chef's . Chef has a big order. is

having a party with **10** guests, and they each want one of his

famous pies!

"Me need to make **10**

pies," says. "It easy to

remember **10**. Me have

10 ."

picture key

pizza	Cookie Monster	hat	Grover	ten	fingers

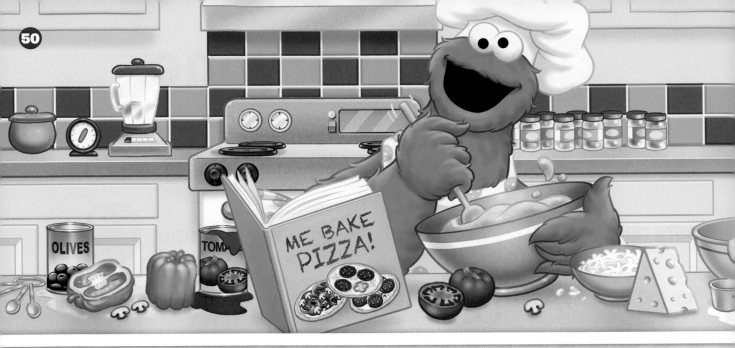

 50

First, Chef makes **10** crusts. He measures **10** cups of flour and pours in **10** cups of water. He divides the dough into **10** pieces, and tosses them in the air **10** times.

Next, Chef tops the **10** pies. He slices **10** 🍄, pours **10** cups of 🥫, and chops **10** chunks of 🧀.

Last, Chef puts the pies in the oven and then sets the ⏲ to **10** minutes.

"See? Me remember **10**," Chef says.

picture key

	10	🍄	🥫	🧀	⏲
Cookie Monster	ten	mushrooms	tomato sauce	cheese	timer

Chef carries each outside and counts, "One, two, three, four, five, six, seven, eight, nine, ...huh? No for me? Me need one more  so me don't forget to count ME!"

"You can have a slice of my ," says .

"And mine," says .

Everyone shares a slice of with . He ends up with 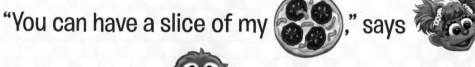 slices!

"That lot of ," says . "Even for me."

Look and Find

"Ah ah ah! Let's count some foods that make a colorful sight. Quick, before these shoppers stop and take a great big bite!"

1 blue food

2 yellow foods

2 purple foods

2 red foods

2 orange foods

3 green foods

Shapes and Colors

 Gets in Shape

Hello, everybodee! I, Professor , am here to teach you about something that is all around you: shapes! This is a shape. It is a shape, which means it has four straight sides (usually two long and two short) and four angles. This is a  too. And so is this . And guess what? The you are holding is a , too!

picture key

 Grover

door

rectangle

window

mirror

book

Even  likes shapes...well, shapes that are in and around

his , like this tossed-out slice of . The  is shaped

like a 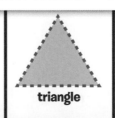, which means it has three sides and three angles.

This half of a  is also a 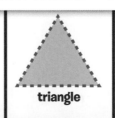 shape. And this

slice looks like a 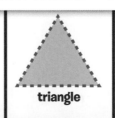, too. But not for long, because I am going

to take a big bite out of it! Bye-bye, 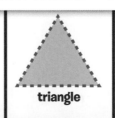.

picture key

| Oscar | trash can | pizza | triangle | sandwich | watermelon |

Now it is time for some 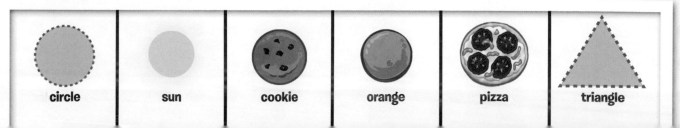-shaped fun in the ( ) . A ( ) is round and has no pointy angles. This (cookie) is a ( ), and this (orange) is a ( ), and this (pizza) pie is a ( ) too.

Wait a minute: (pizza) can be a (triangle) OR a ( )? Is there anything (pizza) cannot do? That reminds me of another question.

What did the ( ) say to the (triangle)? "I see your point." Ha-ha!

picture key

circle	sun	cookie	orange	pizza	triangle

WHAT'S DIFFERENT?

I, Grover, think green is keen! Can you find 10 things
that are different between one green scene and the other?

Sing and Dance

Joins the Band

 is learning about music at school.  loves music.

He wants to be the lead singer in a rock 'n' roll band. will

play the . Rat-a-tat! will play the . Ring-a-ling!

 will sing on a great big stage.

"Some , a singer, and one measly ?" says .

"You call that a rock 'n' roll band? Scram!"

picture key

Oscar	Elmo	Cookie Monster	drums	Zoe	tambourine

64

 loves music too. He wants to be the leader of a big band.  will play the . Fiddle-dee-dee!

will play the . Oompah-oompah!  will tap out the

time while they play.

"A  and a ?" says . "That's the littlest big

band I ever heard of. Hey, didn't I say scram?"

picture key

| Big Bird | Bert | violin | Ernie | bassoon | Oscar |

 and  start to scram, but as they do  steps on something shiny. It's a .

", is this your ?"  asks.

"As a matter of fact, it is,"  says.

"Do you want to be in one of our bands?"  asks.

"Well, I was kinda busy," says .

"But if you insist. I should mention that I play  and  too."

picture key

Big Bird	Elmo	horn	Oscar	tambourine	maracas

Look and Find

The toe-tapping Twiddlebugs
are ready to spin.
And a-one, and a-two!
Bert counts them in.

Can you count these things
on the stage?

1 trumpet

2 Twiddlebugs

3 spotlights

4 cello strings

5 music notes

A Hike on

"**W**hat should we do today?" asks  .

"Oh, why don't you all take a hike!" says  .

"Good idea!" says  . "Let's take a *nature* hike!"

 wonders if they should hike in the forest or on a farm.

"We can take a nature hike right here on  !" says  .

"Aw, who needs nature when you can have ?"  growls.

"Go on, scram!"

picture key

Sesame Street	Ernie	Oscar	Zoe	Grover	trash

"How will we find nature on ?" asks .

"Look at the on these doors," says. "The ivy is growing

way up to the sky. And I see a ! A city and

are right at home on ."

" may not be a forest," says , "but see that ? And

those bee-yootiful ?"

"The like the too," says . "Hi, little guys."

picture key

Sesame Street	Grover	leaves	Bert	bird
Big Bird	tree	flowers	butterflies	Ernie

"This city-grown 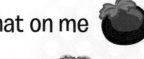 look mighty tasty," says .

"Om nom nom. Hey, what that on me ?"

"That's our pal !" says . "We're back where we started."

"I thought I told you to take a hike," says .

"We did!" says . "We followed nature up and down , right back here to YOU."

picture key

tomato	Cookie Monster	Slimey	Zoe	Oscar	Sesame Street

Look and Find

Whenever Elmo takes a walk,
he sees his neighbors on the block.
Some have two feet. Some have four.
Some, like bugs, have even more!

Lots of monsters live on Sesame Street.
Lots of animals do, too! Can you
spot these animal friends in the
neighborhood?

Out and About

Where Is ?

U h-oh! can't find his doll anywhere. imagines

where in the he might be.

 likes to play in the water. Has he gone to live in the sea

with the little and  and 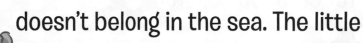?

No, knows doesn't belong in the sea. The little

 and  and  can breathe in water. But

and  need air to breathe.

picture key

Baby David	Elmo	world	fish	sea stars	crabs

 likes to play in the snow. Has he gone to live in Antarctica

with the little ?

No, knows doesn't belong in Antarctica. The little

 are covered with special feathers that keep them warm.

Antarctica is too cold for .

 likes to play in the trees. Has he gone to live in the rainforest

with the little and and ?

Maybe...but wouldn't miss playing with ?

picture key

				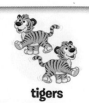	
Baby David	penguins	Elmo	monkeys	tigers	elephants

Suddenly [Elmo] remembers something. He runs up the [stairs] to his room, looks under his [bed]...and finds [Baby David]!

[Elmo] and [Baby David] were under the [bed] pretending to explore a deep, dark cave when [Mommy] called [Elmo] down for dinner.

"Oh, [Baby David], wherever you go in the whole [world]," [Elmo] says, "[Elmo] will go too. You and [Elmo] belong together."

picture key

 **Elmo**   **stairs**   **bed**   **Baby David**   **Mommy**   **world**

WHAT'S DIFFERENT?

Elmo is exploring Australia!
Spot 10 things that are different in these scenes from Down Under.